Annie picked up the book. She stared at the picture on the open page.

"Wow, this place looks great." She showed the picture to Jack.

He saw a sunny beach. A big green parrot sitting in a palm tree. And a ship sailing on a blue sea.

Another gust of rainy wind blew into the tree house.

Annie pointed to the picture. "I wish we were there instead of here," she said.

"Yeah," said Jack. "But where is there?"

"Too late!" came a squawk.

Jack and Annie turned quickly.

Sitting on a branch outside the window ledge of the tree house was a green parrot. Exactly like the parrot in the picture.

*Read all the adventures of **Jack** and **Annie**!*

1. Valley of the Dinosaurs
2. Castle of Mystery
3. Secret of the Pyramid
4. Pirates' Treasure!

Coming soon . . .

5. Night of the Ninjas

Magic Tree House

PIRATES' TREASURE

MARY POPE OSBORNE

Illustrated by Philippe Masson

RED FOX

PIRATES' TREASURE!
A RED FOX BOOK 978 1 782 95383 8

First published in Great Britain by Red Fox,
an imprint of Random House Children's Publishers UK
A Random House Group Company

Published in the US by Random House Children's Books,
a division of Random House Inc, 1992

Red Fox edition published 2008

The Random House Group Limited supports the Forest Stewardship Council®
(FSC®), the leading international forest-certification organisation. Our books
carrying the FSC label are printed on FSC®-certified paper. FSC is the only
forest-certification scheme supported by the leading environmental organisations,
including Greenpeace. Our paper procurement policy can be found at
www.randomhouse.co.uk/environment

MIX
Paper from
responsible sources
FSC® C016897

Set in Bembo Schoolbook

Red Fox Books are published by Random House Children's Publishers UK,
61–63 Uxbridge Road, London W5 5SA

www.kidsatrandomhouse.co.uk

Addresses for companies within The Random House Group Limited can be found at:
www.randomhouse.co.uk/offices.htm

THE RANDOM HOUSE GROUP Limited Reg. No. 954009

A CIP catalogue record for this book is available from the British Library.

Printed and bound by CPI Group (UK) Ltd, Croydon, CR0 4YY

For Andrew Kim Boyce

Contents

1

Too Late!

Jack stared out of his bedroom window. The rain kept falling. And falling.

"The TV said it would stop by midday," said Annie, his seven-year-old sister.

"It's already past midday," said Jack.

"But we have to go to the tree house," said Annie. "I have a feeling the M person will be there today."

Jack pushed his glasses into place and took a deep breath. He wasn't sure he was ready to meet the M person yet. The

mysterious person who had put all the
books in the magic tree house.

"Come on," said Annie.

Jack sighed. "OK," he said. "You get
our waterproofs and wellies. I'll get the
medallion and bookmark."

Annie ran to get their rain stuff.

Jack reached into his drawer. He
took out the medallion.

It was gold. The letter M was
engraved on it.

Then he took out the
bookmark. It was made of
blue leather. It had the
same M on it.

Both Ms matched the M
that was on the floor of the
tree house.

Jack put the medallion and
bookmark into his rucksack. Then he

threw in his notebook and pencil. Jack liked to take notes about important things.

"I got our rain stuff!" called Annie.

Jack picked up his bag and went downstairs. Annie was waiting by the back door. She was putting on her wellies. "Meet you outside," she said.

Jack pulled on his waterproof and wellies. Then he put on his rucksack and joined her. The wind was blowing hard.

"Ready! Steady! Go!" shouted Annie.

They kept their heads down and charged into the rainy wind.

3

Soon they were in the Frog Valley woods.

Tree branches swayed, flinging rain water everywhere.

"Yuck!" said Annie.

They splashed through puddles. Until they came to the tallest oak tree in the woods.

They looked up.

Tucked between two branches was the tree house. It looked dark and lonely against the stormy sky.

Hanging from the tree house was a rope ladder. It was blowing in the wind.

Jack thought of all the books up there. He hoped they weren't getting wet.

"The M person's been there," said Annie.

Jack caught his breath. "How can you tell?" he said.

"I can feel it," she whispered.

She grabbed the rope ladder and started up. Jack followed.

Inside the tree house it was chilly and damp.

But the books were dry. They were all neatly stacked along the wall. Just the way they had been the day before.

Annie picked up a castle book on top of one stack. It had taken them to the time of castles.

"Remember the knight?" she said.

Jack nodded. He would never forget the knight who had helped them.

Annie put down the castle book. She picked up the next book on the stack.

It was the dinosaur book that had taken them to the time of dinosaurs.

"Remember?" she said.

Jack nodded.

5

He'd never forget the Pteranodon who had saved him from the Tyrannosaurus rex.

Then Annie held up a book about ancient Egypt.

"Meow," she said.

Jack smiled. The Egypt book had taken them to the time of pyramids. A black cat had come to the rescue there.

"And here's the book about home," Annie said.

She held up the book with the picture of their town in it.

Frog Valley.

Jack smiled again. The Frog Valley book had brought them back home at the end of each of their adventures.

Jack sighed. OK. He still had two main questions.

Who was the M person who had

put all the books here?

And did the knight, the Pteranodon and the cat all know the M person?

Finally Jack reached into his rucksack. He took out the gold medallion and the leather bookmark. He placed them on the floor. Right over the spot where the M glowed faintly in the wood.

Rain blew into the tree house.

"Brr!" said Annie. "It's not very cosy today."

Jack agreed with her. It was too wet and cold.

"Look." Annie pointed to an open book lying in the corner. "I don't remember a book being open."

"Me neither," said Jack.

Annie picked up the book. She stared at the picture on the open page.

"Wow, this place looks great." She showed the picture to Jack.

He saw a sunny beach. A big green parrot sitting in a palm tree. And a ship sailing on a blue sea.

Another gust of rainy wind blew into the tree house.

Annie pointed to the picture. "I wish we were there instead of here," she said.

"Yeah," said Jack. "But where is there?"

"Too late!" came a squawk.

Jack and Annie turned quickly.

Sitting on a branch outside the window ledge of the tree house was a green parrot. Exactly like the parrot in the picture.

"Too late!" the parrot squawked again.

"A talking parrot!" said Annie. "Is your name Polly? Can I call you Polly?"

Suddenly the wind started to whistle.

"Oh no! Now we're in big trouble!" said Jack.

The wind blew harder.

The leaves shook.

The tree house started to spin. Faster and faster!

Jack squeezed his eyes shut. Then everything was still.

Absolutely still.

Jack opened his eyes.

"Too late!" squawked Polly.

2

The Bright Blue Sea

Jack felt hot sunlight streaming into the tree house.

He smelled salt water.

He heard the sound of waves.

He and Annie looked out of the window.

The tree house was in a palm tree. Beyond was a bright blue sea. A tall sailing ship was on the horizon. It was just like the picture in the book.

"Too late!" squawked Polly.

"Look!" said Annie.

Polly was flying in circles above the tree house. Then she swooped down to the sea.

"Come on, let's follow her! Let's go in the water!" said Annie. She took off her waterproof and dropped it on the floor.

"Wait, we have to study the book first," said Jack. He started to reach for the book. But Annie grabbed it.

"You can read it on the beach," she said. Without even looking at the cover, she shoved the book into Jack's rucksack.

He sighed. Actually, the water *did* look wonderful.

"OK," Jack said. He took off his waterproof too.

"Come on!" Annie handed Jack his rucksack, then started down the ladder.

Jack folded the waterproof and put it next to the stack of books. He put on his rucksack. Then he went down the ladder.

As soon as Annie hit the sand, she ran towards the sea. Jack watched her wade into the water. She was still wearing her wellies.

"Your wellies, Annie," called Jack.

She shrugged. "They'll dry out," she said.

Jack took off his boots and socks. He put them beside his bag. Then he rolled up his jeans. And ran across the hot sand into the waves.

The water was warm and clear. Jack could see shells and tiny fishes.

He shielded his eyes against the sun. And peered out at the sea.

The tall sailing ship seemed a bit closer.

"Where's Polly?" said Annie.

Jack glanced around. No sign of Polly.

Not in the palm trees. Not on the sunlit
sand. Not over the bright blue sea.

When Jack looked out at the sea
again, the ship seemed even closer. Now
Jack could see its flag.

As he stared at the ship's flag, a chill
went through him.

The flag was black. *With a skull and
crossbones.*

"Oh no," he breathed. He started out of the water.

"What's wrong?" said Annie. She splashed after him.

Jack ran over to his rucksack. Annie followed.

He grabbed the book from his rucksack. He looked at the cover. For the first time, he and Annie read the title of the book.

"Wow!" said Annie.

"*Pirates of the Caribbean*," Jack read aloud.

3

Three Men in a Boat

"We've come to the time of pirates!" Jack said.

"Pirates?" squeaked Annie. "Like in *Peter Pan?*"

Jack flipped to the picture that showed the parrot, the sea and the ship.

He read the caption under the picture:

Three hundred years ago, pirates raided Spanish treasure ships in the Caribbean Sea.

He grabbed his notebook and pencil

from his bag. He wrote:

pirates in the Caribbean

He turned to the next page. There was a picture of a pirate flag. He read:

The skull-and-crossbones flag was called the Jolly Roger.

"Let's go!" said Annie.

"Wait!" said Jack. "I want to do a drawing of the flag."

He propped the pirate book in the sand.

He started drawing the Jolly Roger flag.

"Don't copy the pictures in the book," said Annie. "Look at the real thing."

But Jack pushed his glasses into place and kept drawing.

"Jack, some pirates are getting into a rowing boat," said Annie.

Jack kept drawing.

"Jack, the boat's leaving the big ship," said Annie.

"What?" Jack looked up.

"Look." Annie pointed.

Jack looked. He saw the rowing boat coming towards the shore.

"Run!" said Annie. She started running towards the tree house.

Jack jumped up. His glasses fell off.

"Hurry!" Annie called back to him.

Jack went down on his knees. He felt for his glasses. Where were they?

Jack saw something glinting in the sand. He reached for it. It was his glasses. He snatched them up.

Then he threw his notebook and pencil into his bag. He put the pack on his back.

He grabbed his wellies and his socks. And he set off, running.

"Hurry! They're coming!" Annie was at the top of the rope ladder.

Jack looked back at the sea. The pirates were closer to the shore.

Suddenly Jack saw the pirate book. In all the confusion he had forgotten it. It was still propped in the sand.

"Oh no, I forgot the book!" he said. He dropped his socks and wellies below the tree house.

"Come on, Jack!" Annie shouted.

"I'll be right back!" Jack called. "I've got to get the book!"

"Jack, forget it!"

But Jack was already running towards the water.

Jack grabbed the book.

"Come back!" Annie shouted.

Jack shoved
the book into
his rucksack.

Suddenly a giant wave carried the rowing boat right onto the beach.

"Run, Jack!" shouted Annie.

Three big pirates splashed onto the sand.

They had knives in their teeth.

They had pistols in their belts.

They charged towards Jack.

"Run, Jack, run!" cried Annie.

4

Vile Booty

Jack started to run across the hot sand.
He ran as fast as he could.

But the pirates ran faster.

Before Jack knew it, the biggest pirate
had grabbed him!

Jack struggled. But the pirate had
huge, strong arms. He held onto Jack and
laughed a nasty, ugly laugh. He had a
shaggy black beard. A patch covered one
eye.

Jack heard Annie yelling. He saw her
coming down the rope ladder.

"Stay where you are!" Jack shouted.

But Annie kept coming. "Leave him alone, you bully!" she cried.

The other two pirates laughed nastily. They were dirty and ragged.

Annie charged up to the biggest pirate. "Let him go!" she said. She hit the pirate with her fist and kicked him.

But the pirate just growled. Then he grabbed her, too. And with his giant hands, he held Jack and Annie as if they were two kittens.

"*No* one escapes Cap'n Bones!" he roared. His breath was terrible.

"Let go!" Annie shouted into his face.

But Cap'n Bones just smiled. All his teeth were black.

Annie fell silent.

Cap'n Bones laughed loudly. Then he turned to the other two.

"Find out what's in their house, you dogs," he said.

"Aye, aye, Cap'n!" they answered. And they started up the ladder to the tree house.

"What do you spy, Pinky?" shouted Cap'n Bones.

"Books, Cap'n!" Pinky shouted down.

"Arghh, books," growled Cap'n Bones. He spat on the sand. "I want gold, you dogs!"

"Dogs are nicer than you," said Annie.

"Shhh," said Jack.

"What about you, Stinky?" Cap'n Bones roared.

"Just books, Cap'n!" shouted Stinky.

"Arghh, books," said Cap'n Bones. He spat on the sand again. "I hate books! Keep looking, dogs! Find me something good!"

Cap'n Bones grabbed Jack's rucksack. "What's in here?" he said.

"Nothing—" Jack quickly opened the bag. "Just paper, a pencil, a book."

"Another book!" roared Cap'n Bones. "That's vile booty!"

A gleeful shriek pierced the air.

Cap'n Bones froze. "What's that?" he shouted.

"Look, Cap'n! Look!"

Pinky leaned out of the tree-house window. He held the medallion. It glimmered in the sunlight.

Oh no, thought Jack.

"Throw it down!" cried Cap'n Bones.

"It's not yours!" shouted Annie.

Cap'n Bones dropped Jack and Annie. He caught the medallion as it fell.

"Gold! Gold! Gold!" he cried. Cap'n Bones threw back his head and laughed horribly.

He grabbed two of his pistols. He fired them into the air. Pinky and Stinky howled like wolves.

5

The Kid's Treasure

Jack and Annie watched in horror.

The gold-greedy pirates seemed to have lost their minds.

Jack nudged Annie. Together they started to back slowly away from the pirates. Towards the tree house.

"Halt!" Cap'n Bones shouted. He aimed his pistols at them. "Not another step, lubbers!"

Jack and Annie froze.

Cap'n Bones grinned his black-toothed grin. "Tell old Bones where the rest is," he growled. "Or prepare to meet thy doom."

"What – what rest?" said Annie.

"The rest of the treasure!" roared Cap'n Bones. "I know it's on this island. I have a map!"

He reached into a belt pouch and pulled out a torn piece of paper. He waved it at Jack and Annie.

The gold doth lie beneath the whale's eye.

"Is that a treasure map?" asked Jack.

"Aye, it's the map telling about Kidd's treasure."

"Which kid's treasure? Not *us* kids," said Annie. "We don't know anything about a kid's treasure."

"Why don't you read the map?" said Jack.

"*You* read it!" Cap'n Bones shoved the map in Jack's face.

Jack stared at the strange marks on the paper.

"What does that mean?" he asked.

"What does *what* mean?" asked Cap'n Bones.

"Those words." Jack pointed at the words at the bottom of the map.

"Well, it means . . ." Cap'n Bones's good eye squinted at the writing. He

frowned. He coughed. He rubbed his
nose.

"Aw, leave him alone," Pinky growled
at Jack.

"You know he can't read," said Stinky.

"Shut up!" Cap'n Bones roared at his
men.

"Jack and I can read," Annie piped up.

"Shhh," said Jack.

"Cap'n, make 'em read the map!" said
Stinky.

Cap'n Bones gave Jack and Annie a
dark look. "Read it," he growled.

"Then will you let us go?" said Jack.

The pirate squinted with his good
eye. "Aye, lubber. When the treasure's
in me hands, I'll let you go."

"OK," said Jack. "I'll read it
to you." He looked at the map.
"It says, *The gold doth lie*

beneath the whale's eye."

"Eh?" Cap'n Bones scowled. "What's that supposed to mean, lubber?"

Jack shrugged.

"Hang it! Take 'em back to the ship!" shouted Cap'n Bones. "They can rot there till they're ready to tell us how to find Kidd's treasure!"

Jack and Annie were tossed into the rowing boat.

Waves splashed the sides. The sky ahead was dark with thunderclouds. A strong wind had started to blow.

"Row, dogs, row!" said Cap'n Bones.

Pinky and Stinky began rowing towards the big ship.

"Look!" Annie said to Jack. She pointed to the shore.

Polly the parrot was flying over the sand.

"She wants to help us," whispered Annie.

Polly started to fly out over the waves. But the winds were too strong. She turned round and flew back to the island.

6

The Whale's Eye

The rowing boat tossed from side to side. The waves were huge. Salty spray stung Jack's eyes. He felt seasick.

"Hold 'er steady!" shouted Cap'n Bones.

He pointed at the sea. "Or we'll be meat for those evil brutes!"

Dark fins cut through the water. *Sharks.* One zoomed right by the boat. Jack could have reached out and touched it.

He shuddered.

Soon the rowing boat pulled alongside the ship.

The air was filled with wild fiddle music and bagpipes playing. And Jack heard jeers, shouts and ugly laughter.

"Hoist 'em aboard!" Cap'n Bones shouted to his men.

Annie and Jack were hauled onto the deck.

The ship creaked and moaned. It rolled from side to side. Ropes flapped and snapped in the wild wind.

Everywhere they looked, Jack and Annie saw pirates.

Some were dancing. Some were drinking. Many were fighting. With swords. Or with their fists.

"Lock 'em in my cabin!" Cap'n Bones ordered.

A couple of pirates grabbed Jack and

Annie. And threw them in the ship's
cabin. Then locked the door.

The air inside the cabin was damp and
sour-smelling. A shaft of grey light came
through a small round window.

"Oh no," said Jack. "We've got to figure out how to get back to the island."

"So we can get into the tree house and go home," said Annie.

"Right." Jack suddenly felt tired. How would they ever get out of this mess?

"We better examine the book," he said.

He reached into his bag and pulled out the pirate book.

He flipped through the pages.

He looked for information to help them.

"Look," he said.

He found a picture of pirates burying a treasure chest. "This might help."

Together they read the words under the picture.

Captain Kidd was a famous pirate. It is said that he buried a treasure chest on a deserted island. The chest was filled with gold and jewels.

"Captain Kidd!" said Jack.

"So *that's* the *kid* that Bones keeps talking about," said Annie.

"Right," said Jack.

Annie looked out of the round window.

"And Captain Kidd's treasure is buried somewhere on the island," she said.

Jack took out his notebook and pencil. He wrote:

Captain Kidd's treasure on island

"Ja-ack," Annie said.

"Shhh, wait a minute," he said. "I'm thinking."

"Guess what I see?" said Annie.

"What?" Jack asked. He looked back at the book.

"A whale."

"Neat," he said. Then he looked up. "A whale? Did you say . . . a whale?"

"A whale. A huge whale. As big as a football pitch."

Jack jumped up and looked out of the window with her.

"Where?" he asked. All he could see

was the island. And stormy waves. And shark fins.

"There!" said Annie.

"Where? Where?"

"There! The *island* is shaped like a giant whale!"

"Oh!" whispered Jack. Now he could see it.

"See the whale's back?" said Annie.

"Yes." The slope of the island looked like the back of a whale.

"See his spout?" said Annie.

"Yes." The palm tree that held the tree house looked like the spout of the whale.

"See his eye?" said Annie.

"Yep." A big black rock looked like the eye of the whale.

"*The gold doth lie beneath the whale's eye*," whispered Jack. "Wow."

7
Gale's a-Blowin'

"So the treasure must be under that rock," said Annie.

"Right," said Jack. "Now we just have to get back to the island. We'll show Cap'n Bones where the treasure is. Then while all the pirates are digging, we'll sneak up to the tree house."

"And make a wish to go home," said Annie.

"Right." Jack poked his head out of the round window of the cabin. "Cap'n Bones, sir!" he shouted.

The pirates took up the cry. "Cap'n Bones! Cap'n Bones!"

"Hey?" came a horrible voice.

Cap'n Bones stuck his ugly face through the window. His good eye glared at Jack. "What do you want, lubbers?"

"We're ready to tell the truth, sir," said Jack.

"Go ahead," growled Cap'n Bones.

"We know where Captain Kidd's treasure is."

"Where?"

"We can't just tell you. We have to *show* you," said Annie.

Cap'n Bones gave Annie and Jack a long hard look.

"You'll need a rope," said Jack.

"And shovels," said Annie.

Cap'n Bones growled. Then he roared at his men, "Get some rope and shovels!"

"Aye, aye, Cap'n!"

"Then throw these lubbers in the boat! We're going back to the island!"

"Aye, aye, Cap'n!"

Back in the rowing boat, Jack saw the sky had grown even darker with clouds. The waves were bigger. The wind was howling.

"Gale's a-blowin'!" said Pinky.

"You'll see a gale if I don't get me gold today, by thunder!" Cap'n Bones shouted. "Row, dogs, row!"

The three pirates battled the waves, until the rowing boat reached the island. They all piled onto the shore.

Cap'n Bones grabbed Jack and Annie.

"OK, lubbers," he said. "Now show us where the treasure is."

"There," said Annie. She pointed at the back rock near the tip of the island.

"Under that rock," said Jack.

Cap'n Bones dragged Jack and Annie down the beach to the black rock.

"Get to work!" Cap'n Bones said to Pinky and Stinky.

"What about you?" said Annie.

"Me? Work?" Cap'n Bones chuckled.

Jack gulped. How could they get away from him?

"Don't you think you should help your friends?" he said.

Cap'n Bones gave Jack a horrible grin. "Nay. I'm going to hold you two – till there's treasure in me hands!"

8

Dig, Dogs, Dig

Pinky and Stinky tied their rope around
the big rock.

The wind howled. The two pirates
pulled. And pulled. And pulled.

"They need help!" said Jack.

"Aghh, let the dogs do the work!"
growled Cap'n Bones.

"You're not very nice to them," said Annie.

"Who cares?" roared Cap'n Bones.

"Cap'n! We got it!" shouted Pinky.

They started pulling the rock across
the sand.

"Now let's dig where the rock was," said Jack. "All of us!"

But Cap'n Bones ignored his suggestion.

"Dig, you dogs!" he shouted.

Pinky and Stinky started to dig. The wind blew even harder. There was going to be a thunderstorm.

"Oww! I got sand in me eyes!" Pinky whined.

"Oww! Me back hurts!" Stinky cried.

"Dig!" shouted Cap'n Bones. He held Jack and Annie with one hand. With the other he pulled out the gold medallion.

He tossed it at the two pirates. It fell into the hole.

"Dig for more of these, you swine!" he said.

Squawk!

"Look!" Annie said.

Polly was back! She was circling above them!

"Go back!" she squawked.

Stinky and Pinky looked up at the parrot. They scowled.

"Dig!" shouted Cap'n Bones.

"A big storm is comin', Cap'n!" said Pinky.

"Go back!" said Polly.

"The bird's an omen, Cap'n!" shouted Stinky.

"Dig, you dogs!" cried Cap'n Bones.

"Go back!" squawked Polly.

"The bird's warning us!" shouted Pinky. "We've got to get to the ship before it's too late!"

The two pirates threw down their shovels. They started running towards the rowing boat.

"Mutineers! Come back!" shouted Cap'n Bones. He dragged Jack and Annie down the beach as he ran after his men. "Stop!"

But the pirates kept running. They got to the rowing boat and pushed it into the sea.

"Wait!"
cried Cap'n
Bones.

Pinky and
Stinky jumped
into the boat.
They started
rowing.

"Wait!"
Cap'n Bones
let go of Jack
and Annie. He ran
into the water. "Wait,
you dogs!"

He hauled himself into the
rowing boat.

Then the three pirates disappeared into
the spray of the waves.

"Go back!" squawked Polly.

"She means *us*!" said Annie.

Just then the storm broke over the island. The wind howled. Rain fell in buckets.

"Let's go!" cried Annie.

"Wait! I have to get the medallion!" shouted Jack. He ran to the hole dug by the pirates. He looked down into it.

Even in the dreary light, the medallion was shining.

Big, fat raindrops were falling into the hole, washing away the sand.

Jack saw a patch of wood.

Then the rain cleared away more sand. And Jack saw the top of an old trunk.

He stared. Was it Captain Kidd's treasure chest?

"Hurry, Jack!" cried Annie. She was halfway up the tree-house ladder.

"I found it! I found it!" cried Jack. "I

found the treasure chest!"

"Forget the treasure chest!" said Annie.
"We have to go now! The storm's getting
worse!"

Jack kept staring at the chest. Was there gold inside? Silver? Precious gems?

"Come on!" Now Annie was shouting from the tree-house window.

But Jack couldn't tear himself away. He brushed the rest of the muddy sand off the chest.

"Jack, forget the treasure chest!" cried Annie. "Let's go!"

"Go back!" squawked Polly.

Jack looked at the parrot. She was perched on the black rock.

He stared into her wise eyes. He thought he knew her – knew her from somewhere else.

"Go back, Jack," she said. She sounded like a person.

OK. It was definitely time to go.

Jack took one last look at the treasure chest. He clutched the gold medallion. Then he set off, running towards the tree house.

His socks and wellies were still there. He quickly pulled the wellies on. He shoved the socks into his rucksack.

The rope ladder was dancing wildly in the wind. Jack grabbed it.

The ladder swayed as Jack climbed. He was tossed this way and that. But he held on tight.

At last he pulled himself into the tree house.

"Let's go!" he cried.

Annie was already holding the Frog Valley book. She pointed to the picture of the woods.

"I wish we could go there!" she shouted.

The wind was already blowing hard. But now it blew even harder.

The tree house started to spin. It spun faster and faster.

Then everything was still.

Absolutely still.

9
The Mysterious M

Drip, drip.

Jack opened his eyes. Rain was dripping from the leaves of the tree.

They were back in Frog Valley. The rain was softer. The wind was gentler. The air was sweeter.

Jack sighed. "That was close." He was still holding the gold medallion.

"Polly's gone," said Annie sadly. "I was hoping she might come back with us."

"No magic creature has ever come back with us," said Jack.

He pulled off his rucksack. It was damp with rain and salt water.

Jack took out the pirate book. He put it on the stack of books. On top of the dinosaur book. And the knight book. And the mummy book.

Then Jack put the gold medallion beside the bookmark with the letter M.

Next he went down onto his knees. And ran his finger over the shimmering M on the floor. "We didn't find any Ms on this trip," he said.

"Or the M person," said Annie.

Squawk!

"Polly!" Annie cried.

The parrot swooshed into the tree house. She perched on the stack of books.

Polly looked straight at Jack.

"What – what are you doing here?" he asked her.

Slowly Polly raised her bright green wings. They grew bigger and bigger until they spread out like a huge green cape.

Then, in a great swirl of colours – in a blur of feathers and light – in a flapping and stretching and screeching – a new being took shape.

Polly was not a parrot any longer. In her place was an old woman. An old woman with long white hair and piercing eyes.

She wore a green feathered cape. She perched on the stack of books. And she was very calm and very still.

Neither Jack nor Annie could speak. They were too amazed.

"Hello, Jack. Hello, Annie," the old woman said. "My name is Morgan le Fay."

10

Treasure Again

Annie found her voice first. "The M person," she whispered.

"Yes. I'm the M person," said Morgan.

"Wh-where are you from?" asked Jack.

"Have you ever heard of King Arthur?" said Morgan.

Jack nodded.

"Well, I am King Arthur's sister," said Morgan.

"You're from Camelot," said Jack. "I've read about Camelot."

"What did you read about me, Jack?" said Morgan.

"You – you're a witch."

Morgan smiled. "You can't believe *everything* you read, Jack."

"But are you a magician?" said Annie.

"Most call me an enchantress. But I'm also a librarian," said Morgan.

"A librarian?" said Annie.

"Yes. And I've come to your time to collect books. You are lucky to be born in a time with so many books."

"For the Camelot library?" asked Jack.

"Precisely," said Morgan. "I travel in this tree house to collect words from many different places around the world. And from many different time periods."

"Did you find books here?" said Jack.

"Oh yes. Many wonderful books. I want to borrow them for our scribes to copy."

"Did you put all the bookmarks in them?" said Jack.

"Yes. You see, I like the pictures in the books. Sometimes I want to visit the scenes in the pictures. So all the bookmarks mark places I wish to go."

"How do you get there?" asked Annie.

"I placed a spell on the tree house," said Morgan. "So when I point to a picture and make the wish, the tree house takes me there."

"I think you dropped this in dinosaur times," said Jack.

He handed the gold medallion to Morgan.

"Oh, thank you! I wondered where I'd lost it," she said. She put the medallion into a hidden pocket in her cape.

"So can anybody work the spell?" asked Annie. "Anybody who tries it?"

"Oh dear, no! Not just anybody," Morgan said. "You two are the only ones besides me to do it. No one else has ever even seen my tree house before."

"Is it invisible?" asked Annie.

"Yes," said Morgan. "I had no idea it would ever be discovered. But then you two came along. Somehow you hooked right into my magic."

"H-how?" asked Jack.

"Well, for two reasons, I think," explained Morgan. "First, Annie believes in magic. So she actually saw the tree house. And her belief helped you to see it, Jack."

"Oh wow," said Jack.

"Then you picked up a book, Jack. And because you love books so much, you caused my magic spell to work."

"Wow," said Annie.

"You can't imagine my dismay when you started to take off for dinosaur times. I had to make a very quick decision. And I decided to come along."

"Oh, so you were the Pteranodon!" said Annie.

Morgan smiled.

"And the cat and the knight and Polly!" said Annie.

"Yes," said Morgan softly.

"You were all these things to help us?" asked Jack.

"Yes, but I must go home now. The people in Camelot need my help."

"You're leaving?" whispered Jack.

"I'm afraid I must," said Morgan.

She picked up Jack's rucksack and handed it to him. Jack and Annie picked up their waterproofs. It had stopped raining.

"You won't forget us, will you?" asked Annie, as they put their waterproofs on.

"Never," said Morgan. She smiled at both of them. "You remind me too much of myself. You love the impossible, Annie. And you love knowledge, Jack. What better combination is there?"

Morgan le Fay touched Annie's forehead gently. And then Jack's. She smiled.

"Goodbye," she said.

"Goodbye," said Annie and Jack.

Annie left the tree house first. Jack followed. They climbed down the rope ladder for the last time.

They stood below the oak tree and looked up.

Morgan was looking out of the window. Her long white hair blew in the breeze.

Suddenly the wind began to blow.

The leaves began to shake.

A loud whistling sound filled the air.

Jack covered his ears and squeezed his eyes shut.

Then everything was silent.

Absolutely silent.

Jack opened his eyes.

The tree house was gone.

All gone.

Absolutely gone.

Annie and Jack stood for a moment, staring up at the empty oak tree. Listening to the silence.

Annie sighed. "Let's go," she said softly.

Jack just nodded. He felt too sad to speak. As they starting walking, he put his hands into his pockets.

He felt something.

Jack pulled out the gold medallion. "Look!" he said. "How did—?"

Annie smiled. "Morgan must have put it there," she said.

"But how?"

"Magic," said Annie. "I think it means she'll be coming back."

Jack smiled. He clutched the medallion as he and Annie headed off through the wet, sunny woods.

As they walked, the sun shone through the woods. And all the wet leaves sparkled.

Everything, in fact, was shining.

Leaves, branches, puddles, bushes, grass, vines, wild flowers — all glittered like jewels.

Or gleamed like gold.

Annie had been right, thought Jack.

Forget the treasure chest.

They had treasure at home. Lots of it. Everywhere.

Magic Tree House

NIGHT OF THE NINJAS

Mary Pope Osborne

*Climb the ladder to the Magic Tree House.
There's a world of adventure inside!*

Jack and Annie's adventures
have started again!

They're stuck in ancient Japan,
where the shadowy ninjas and the
fierce Samurai warriors don't look very
friendly! Will Jack and Annie find the
tree house again? Or will they be
caught in a terrifying battle?

ISBN: 978 1 862 30566 3